THE LITTLE ENGINE THAT COULD

RETOLD BY
WATTY PIPER
REIMAGINED BY
DAN SANTAT

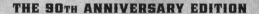

THE 90TH ANNIVERSARY EDITION

PLATT & MUNK

READING TIPS FOR SHARING BOOKS WITH YOUR CHILD

Here are some ways to get the most out of reading *The Little Engine That Could* and other books with your child:

- Follow your child's lead. If your baby is staring at an object or picture, talk about it. Say, "What do you see? Is that a bear? It's a brown, furry bear." (infant)

- Ask your child to point to and name pictures. Ask, "Where is the clown?" or "What animal is this?" (toddler)

- Ask questions about the story. "How do you think the Little Engine feels as she goes up the mountain?" Pause and wait for your child to answer. (preschooler)

- Use the pictures to teach new words. Say, "See the railroad track? A track is a road for a train." (all ages)

Here are some ways you can extend your child's learning "on the go":

- Bring books to read while you wait in line at the store or at the doctor's office.

- Choose a word or phrase from the books you've read and use it throughout the day. As you push the stroller up the hill, say, "I think I can, I think I can."

Hello Dear Friends,

Welcome to the Imagination Library! This wonderful book, *The Little Engine That Could*, is just the first of many more books to come because of the support of local sponsors like the one listed on this book's mailing label. I hope every book brings joy to your entire family, because I am certain that if you love books you will love learning.

I want to share a few lines of a song I wrote for the Imagination Library. The song is called "Try."

Try to be the first one up the mountain,
The highest flying dreamer in the sky.
Try your best to be an inspiration
For others that are still afraid and shy.
Try to make the most of every moment
If you fail get up and try again.
Try each day a little harder
If you never try, you never win.

As a special gift to you, I wanted to also gift a free download from my children's CD titled "I Believe in You." Maybe you will have as much fun listening to it as I did writing it. Just look down below for a link to download this free song. The only thing I ask for in return is for you to read these books as often as you possibly can. Now that is what I call a good deal!

Love,

Dolly Parton

You can download the free song from Dolly's CD "I Believe in You" by visiting: imaginationlibrary.com/music

GROSSET & DUNLAP

An Imprint of Penguin Random House LLC, New York

Text copyright © 1976, 1961, 1954, 1945, 1930 by Penguin Random House LLC. Illustrations copyright © 2020 by
Penguin Random House LLC. All rights reserved. This 90th Anniversary Edition published in 2020 by Platt & Munk, Publishers,
an imprint of Grosset & Dunlap. The Little Engine That Could®, I Think I Can®, and all related titles, logos, and characters are trademarks
of Penguin Random House LLC. GROSSET & DUNLAP is a registered trademark of Penguin Random House LLC. Manufactured in China.

Visit us online at www.penguinrandomhouse.com.

Library of Congress Cataloging-in-Publication Data is available upon request.

ISBN 9780593094396
Special Markets ISBN 9780593222805
Not for Resale
11
Text set in Century Schoolbook.

This Imagination Library edition is published by
Penguin Young Readers Group, a division of Penguin Random House,
exclusively for Dolly Parton's Imagination Library, a not-for-profit
program designed to inspire a love of reading and learning,
sponsored in part by The Dollywood Foundation. Penguin's trade
editions of this work are available wherever books are sold.

THE LITTLE ENGINE THAT COULD

RETOLD BY
WATTY PIPER

REIMAGINED BY
DAN SANTAT

◆——◇——◆

THE 90TH ANNIVERSARY EDITION

PLATT & MUNK

Chug, chug, chug. Puff, puff, puff. Ding-dong, ding-dong. The little train rumbled over the tracks.

She was a happy little train for she had such a jolly load to carry. Her cars were filled full of good things for boys and girls.

There were toy animals—giraffes with long necks, Teddy bears with almost no necks at all, and even a baby elephant.

Then there were dolls—dolls with blue eyes and yellow curls, dolls with brown eyes and brown bobbed heads, and the funniest little toy clown you ever saw.

And there were cars full of toy engines, airplanes, tops, jackknives, picture puzzles, books, and every kind of thing boys or girls could want.

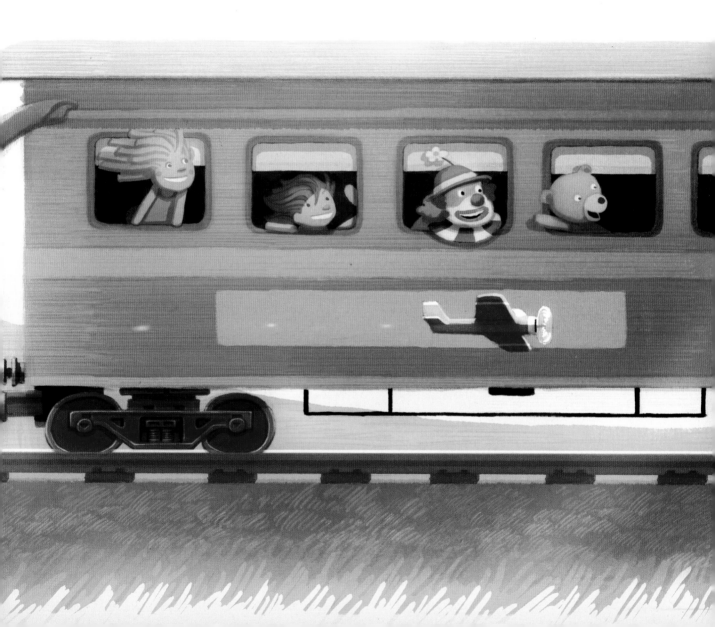

But that was not all. Some of the cars were filled with all sorts of good things for boys and girls to eat—big golden oranges, red-cheeked apples, bottles of creamy milk for their breakfasts, fresh spinach for their dinners, peppermint drops, and lollypops for after-meal treats.

The little train was carrying all these wonderful things to the good little boys and girls on the other side of the mountain.

She puffed along merrily. Then all of a sudden she stopped with a jerk. She simply could not go another inch. She tried and she tried, but her wheels would not turn.

What were all those good little boys and girls on the other side of the mountain going to do without the wonderful toys to play with and the good food to eat?

"Here comes a shiny new engine," said the funny little clown who jumped out of the train. "Let us ask him to help us."

So all the dolls and toys cried out together, "Please, Shiny New Engine, won't you please pull our train over the mountain? Our engine has broken down, and the boys and girls on the other side won't have any toys to play with or good food to eat unless you help us."

But the Shiny New Engine snorted: "I pull you? I am a Passenger Engine. I have just carried a fine big train over the mountain, with more cars than you ever dreamed of. My train had sleeping cars, with comfortable berths; a dining car where waiters bring whatever hungry people want to eat; and parlor cars in which people sit in soft armchairs and look out of big plate-glass windows. I pull the likes of you? Indeed not!"

And off he steamed to the roundhouse, where engines live when they are not busy. How sad the little train and all the dolls and toys felt!

Then the little clown called out, "The Passenger Engine is not the only one in the world. Here is another engine coming, a great big strong one. Let us ask him to help us."

The little toy clown waved his flag and the big strong engine came to a stop.

"Please, oh, please, Big Engine," cried all the dolls and toys together. "Won't you please pull our train over the mountain? Our engine has broken down, and the good little boys and girls on the other side won't have any toys to play with or good food to eat unless you help us."

But the Big Strong Engine bellowed: "I am a Freight Engine. I have just pulled a big train loaded with big machines over the mountain. These machines print books and newspapers for grown-ups to read. I am a very important engine indeed. I won't pull the likes of you!" And the Freight Engine puffed off indignantly to the roundhouse.

The little train and all the dolls and toys were very sad.

"Cheer up," cried the little toy clown. "The Freight Engine is not the only one in the world. Here comes another. He looks very old and tired, but our train is so little, perhaps he can help us."

So the little toy clown waved his flag and the dingy, rusty old engine stopped.

"Please, Kind Engine," cried all the dolls and toys together. "Won't you please pull our train over the mountain? Our engine has broken down, and the boys and girls on the other side won't have any toys to play with or good food to eat unless you help us."

But the Rusty Old Engine sighed, "I am so tired. I must rest my weary wheels. I cannot pull even so little a train as yours over the mountain. I can not. I can not. I can not."

And off he rumbled to the roundhouse chugging, "I can not. I can not. I can not."

Then indeed the little train was very, very sad, and the dolls and toys were ready to cry.

But the little clown called out, "Here is another engine coming, a little blue engine, a very little one, maybe she will help us."

The very little engine came chug, chugging merrily along. When she saw the toy clown's flag, she stopped quickly.

"What is the matter, my friends?" she asked kindly.

"Oh, Little Blue Engine," cried the dolls and toys. "Will you pull us over the mountain? Our engine has broken down and the good boys and girls on the other side won't have any toys to play with or good food to eat, unless you help us. Please, please help us, Little Blue Engine."

"I'm not very big," said the Little Blue Engine. "They use me only for switching trains in the yard. I have never been over the mountain."

"But we must get over the mountain before the children awake," said all the dolls and the toys.

The very little engine looked up and saw the tears in the dolls' eyes. And she thought of the good little boys and girls on the other side of the mountain who would not have any toys or good food unless she helped.

Then she said, "I think I can. I think I can. I think I can."
And she hitched herself to the little train.

She tugged and pulled and pulled and tugged and slowly,
slowly, slowly they started off.

The toy clown jumped aboard and all the dolls and the toy animals began to smile and cheer.

Puff, puff, chug, chug, went the Little Blue Engine. "I think I can—I think I can—I think I can—I think I can—I think I can—I think I can—I think I can— I think I can—I think I can."

Up, up, up. Faster and faster and faster the little engine climbed, until at last they reached the top of the mountain.

Down in the valley lay the city.

"Hurray, hurray," cried the funny little clown and all the
dolls and toys. "The good little boys and girls in the city will
be happy because you helped us, kind Little Blue Engine."

And the Little Blue Engine smiled and seemed to say
as she puffed steadily down the mountain . . .
"I thought I could. I thought I could. I thought I could.
I thought I could. I thought I could. I thought I could."

Dear Friends,

Twenty-five years ago, I decided to offer a free book gifting program to the children in my hometown. For every child's first book from the Imagination Library, we wanted a book that everyone knew, but most of all, a book everyone loved. For most people, this may seem like a difficult choice, but for me, it only took a minute to choose *The Little Engine That Could* to be that very special book.

My memories take me way back to a little cabin in East Tennessee. This was not a place where dreams easily came true. Too often, there was talk about all of the things we couldn't do rather than all of the things we could do. On many occasions, when my dreams seemed far away, my Mama would tell me the story of the Little Engine to comfort and encourage me. While I listened to her, I would close my eyes and think of myself as the Little Engine and just start saying over and over again, "I think I can. I think I can. I think I can." It gave me strength, it gave me hope, and it gave me the courage to keep chasing my dreams.

We have worked with our local partners to gift over five million copies of *The Little Engine That Could* to children all over the United States and Canada. This is an impressive number, but *The Little Engine* is much more than just a book in a child's hands. It is an expression of our love, to ignite the aspirations of children to be whomever they want to be.

So thank you, Little Engine, for inspiring me and for inspiring generations of children for ninety years. May you keep chuggin' along to take all of us to the other side of the mountain!

Love,

Dolly

Dolly Parton

"I think I can."

This simple mantra, which has lasted ninety years, has taught multiple generations of children and adults everywhere that they can possibly achieve something if they just believe in themselves.

I remember my first time reading *The Little Engine That Could* in preschool. There was a hopeful optimism to the story that my impressionable young mind could relate to. It was a lesson in self-confidence. As I grew older, I would occasionally say "I think I can" to myself in jest while preparing for a big test in high school, and then later in college.

Usually with positive results.

Me, an adult male, repeating four little words from a children's story about a tiny blue engine that no one believed in, except for a handful of toys and herself, chanting:

"I think I can. I think I can. I think I can."

It's the voice in your head that gives you permission to believe in yourself when no one else does. A quiet place in your mind where no one can contest your beliefs. The meter of the phrase is balanced, meditative, even calming. You become hypnotized by the rhythm of the phrase, which feels almost as natural as breathing. It's when you are at your best. Over the years I realized that if you say something often enough, you can sometimes convince yourself that it can be done. Today, I still say it to myself before presenting to hundreds of children at schools all over the country, or in the midst of meeting a tight deadline.

It doesn't take much to lift a person's spirits and make us believe that we can all possibly become more than we ever dreamed, and it's all thanks to a little blue train.

Love,

Dan Santat

Dan Santat